For my dearest Rikka

First U.S. miniature edition 1993
First published in Great Britain in 1992
by Walker Books Ltd., London.

Library of Congress Cataloging-in-Publication Data
Alborough, Jez.
Where's my teddy? / Jez Alborough.

Summary: When a small boy named Eddie
goes searching for his lost teddy in the dark woods,
he comes across a gigantic bear with a similar problem.
[1. Teddy bears — Fiction. 2. Bears — Fiction.
3. Stories in rhyme.] I. Title.
PZ8.3.A24Wh   1992
[E] — dc20   91-58765
ISBN 1-56402-255-2 (miniature)

10 9 8 7 6 5 4 3 2 1

The pictures in this book were done
in watercolor, crayon, and pencil.

Printed and bound in Singapore

Candlewick Press
2067 Massachusetts Avenue
Cambridge, Massachusetts 02140

WHERE'S MY TEDDY?

To Erin,
Happy Birthday!
Love,
Savannah

by Jez Alborough

CANDLEWICK PRESS
CAMBRIDGE, MASSACHUSETTS

Eddie's off to find his teddy.
Eddie's teddy's name is Freddie.

He lost him in the woods somewhere.
It's dark and horrible in there.

"Help!" said Eddie. "I'm scared already!
I want my bed! I want my teddy!"

He tiptoed
on and on
until . . .

something
made him stop
quite still.

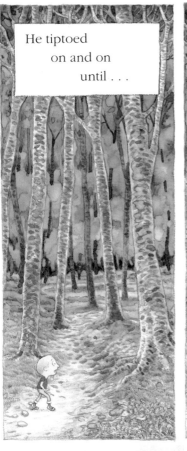

"You're too big to huddle and cuddle," he said,

"and I'll never fit both of us into my bed."

Then out of the darkness,
clearer and clearer,
the sound of sobbing
came nearer and nearer.

Soon the whole woods
could hear the voice bawl,
"How did you get to be
tiny and small?
You're too small to
huddle and cuddle," it said,
"and you'll only get lost
in my giant-sized bed!"

It was a gigantic bear
and a tiny teddy
stomping toward . . .

the giant teddy and Eddie.

"MY TED!"
gasped the bear.
"A BEAR!"
screamed Eddie.

"A BOY!"
yelled the bear.
"MY TEDDY!"
cried Eddie.

Then they ran and they ran
through the dark woods
back to their homes
as fast as they could . . .

all the way back
to their snuggly beds,
where they huddled
and cuddled their
own little teds.